MW00903077

Published by Picture Book Studio, Saxonville, MA.
Distributed in Canada by Vanwell Publishing, St. Catharines, Ont.

Printed in Hong Kong.
10 9 8 7 6 5 4 3 2 1

Library of Congress Cataloging in Publication Data
Carrier, Lark, 1947–
A perfect spring / written and illustrated by Lark Carrier.
Summary: Although the abandoned egg picked up and hatched by Mr. and Mrs. Seabird yields a turtle unlike the baby bird from their own egg, the lessons they have to impart seem to apply to both young creatures equally.
ISBN 0-88708-131-2
[1. Birds—Fiction. 2. Turtles—Fiction. 3. Parent and child—Fiction. I. Title.
PZ7.C23453Pe 1990
[E]—dc20 89-49262

Ask your bookseller for these other **Picture Book Studio** books by Lark Carrier:
There Was a Hill...
Scout and Cody
A Christmas Promise
Do Not Touch
Snowy Path

A Perfect Spring

Lark Carrier

Picture Book Studio

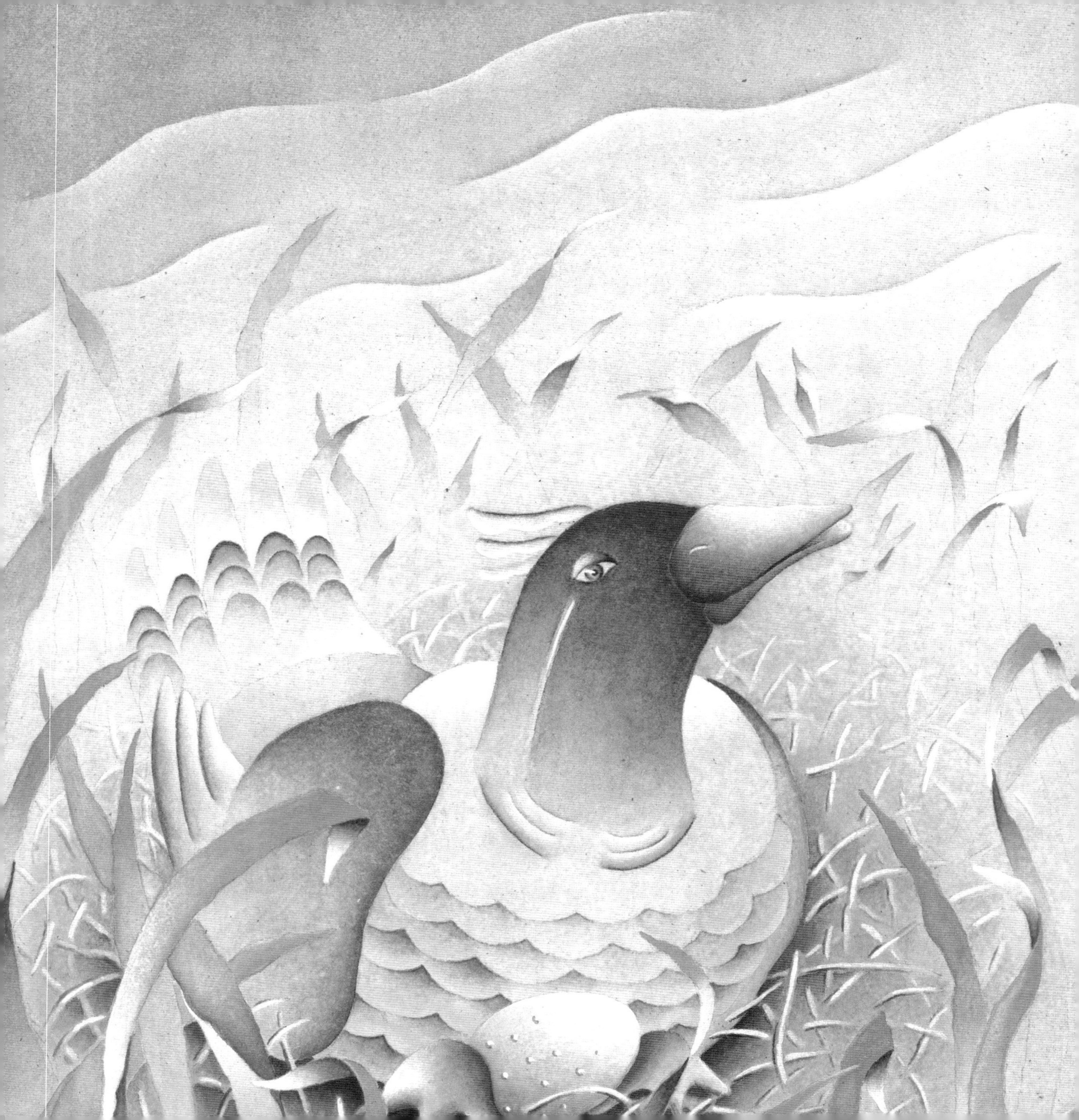

Early each spring Mrs. Seabird lays two eggs.

But this year there is only one, and Mr. and Mrs. Seabird are surprised and disappointed. Since the nest was ready for two eggs, they decide to rebuild it to fit just one.

While searching for smaller twigs among the tall grass, Mr. Seabird screeches for Mrs. Seabird. "Hurry, come see what I've found."

There, half buried in the sandy soil is a beautiful egg—without a nest!

"The perfect solution," cries Mrs. Seabird. "Let's roll it home."

Up and up they push! Down and down it rolls! After a lot of pushing, there it lies next to the other egg. It makes the nest look and feel just right.

Mr. and Mrs. Seabird snuggle on their full nest to begin their long wait for hatching day. "What a perfect spring it will be," sings Mr. Seabird.

Scritch! Scritch! Crack! is the early morning sound as the first egg pops open.
A tiny, feathery head pokes out, and there is Bertie.

Scritch! Scritch! Rrriiip! is the sound as the second egg bursts open. A tiny, shiny head pokes out, and there is Sandy.

Time to eat and grow, and time to learn and think. Mr. and Mrs. Seabird are very happy and busy. They fly back and forth, back and forth, feeding and teaching their two perfect hatchlings.

And they never notice that when Bertie and Sandy listen to their lessons about the future, one always looks up, and one always looks down.

After waiting and waiting, the most exciting and scary day of their lives finally arrives: Bertie and Sandy have learned all their lessons, and they are ready to leave the nest and go off on their own for a whole day.

Up! Up! looks Bertie, and reaching for the sky, he glides away on the swift current.

Down! Down! looks Sandy, and stretching for the sea, he glides away on the swift current.

What a wonderful feeling—gliding up, down, all around, weightless and boundless.

They look at the whole wide world around them. They see a horse, a snake, colorful plants—things flying and running and crawling and blowing all over the place. Everything is just as their parents had said, but more beautiful.

Hungrier than ever before, they test their hunting skills.

With a nose dive down to the earth, they scratch with strong sharp toes, and up comes a feast of delicious morsels.

Bertie and Sandy feel dizzy and tired from so much traveling, but they remember to land on outstretched limbs for shelter and rest.

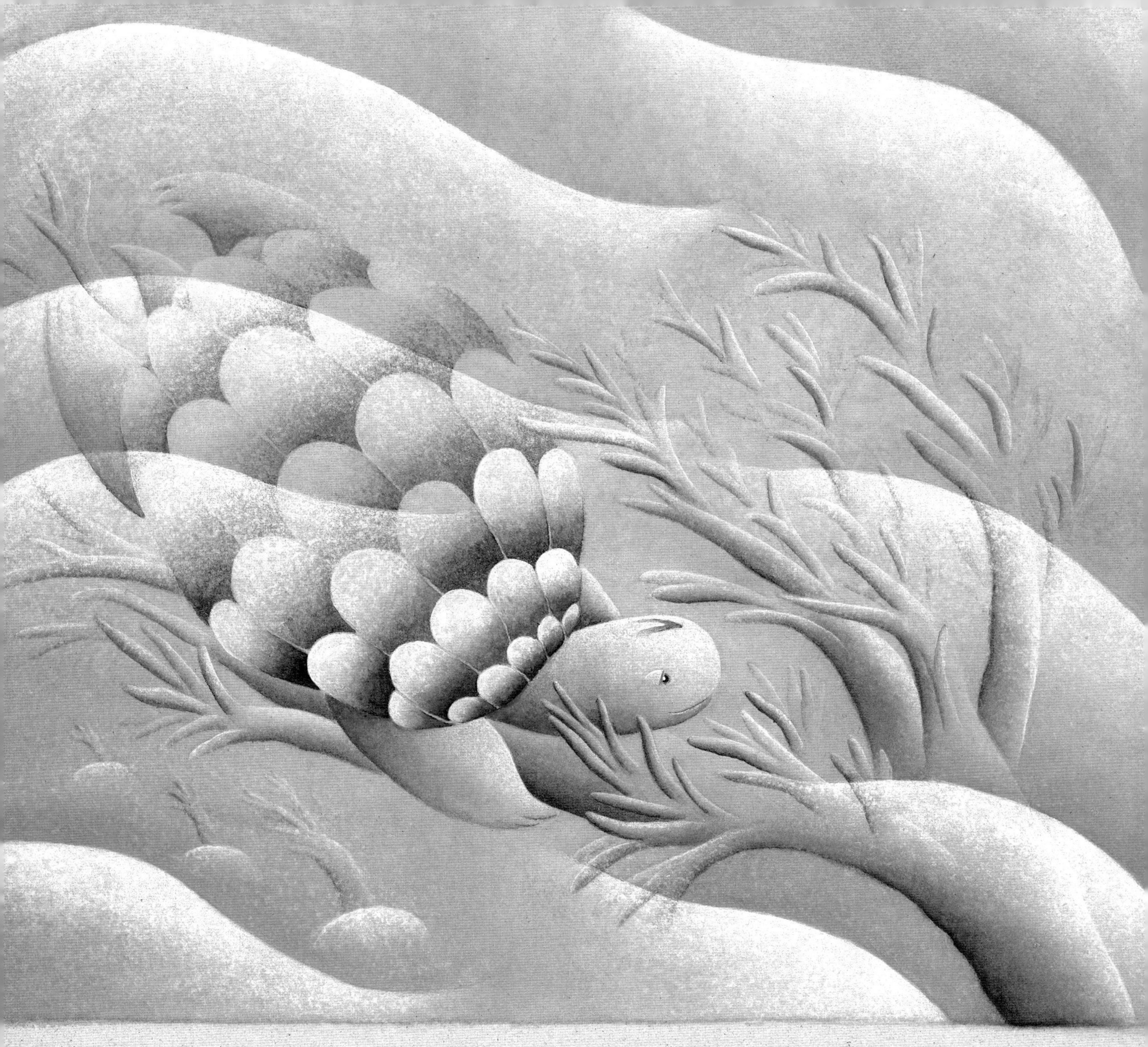

Holding tight, they enjoy the lullabye of the swaying branches.

The day passes quickly, and suddenly it is nighttime. At first they are frightened.

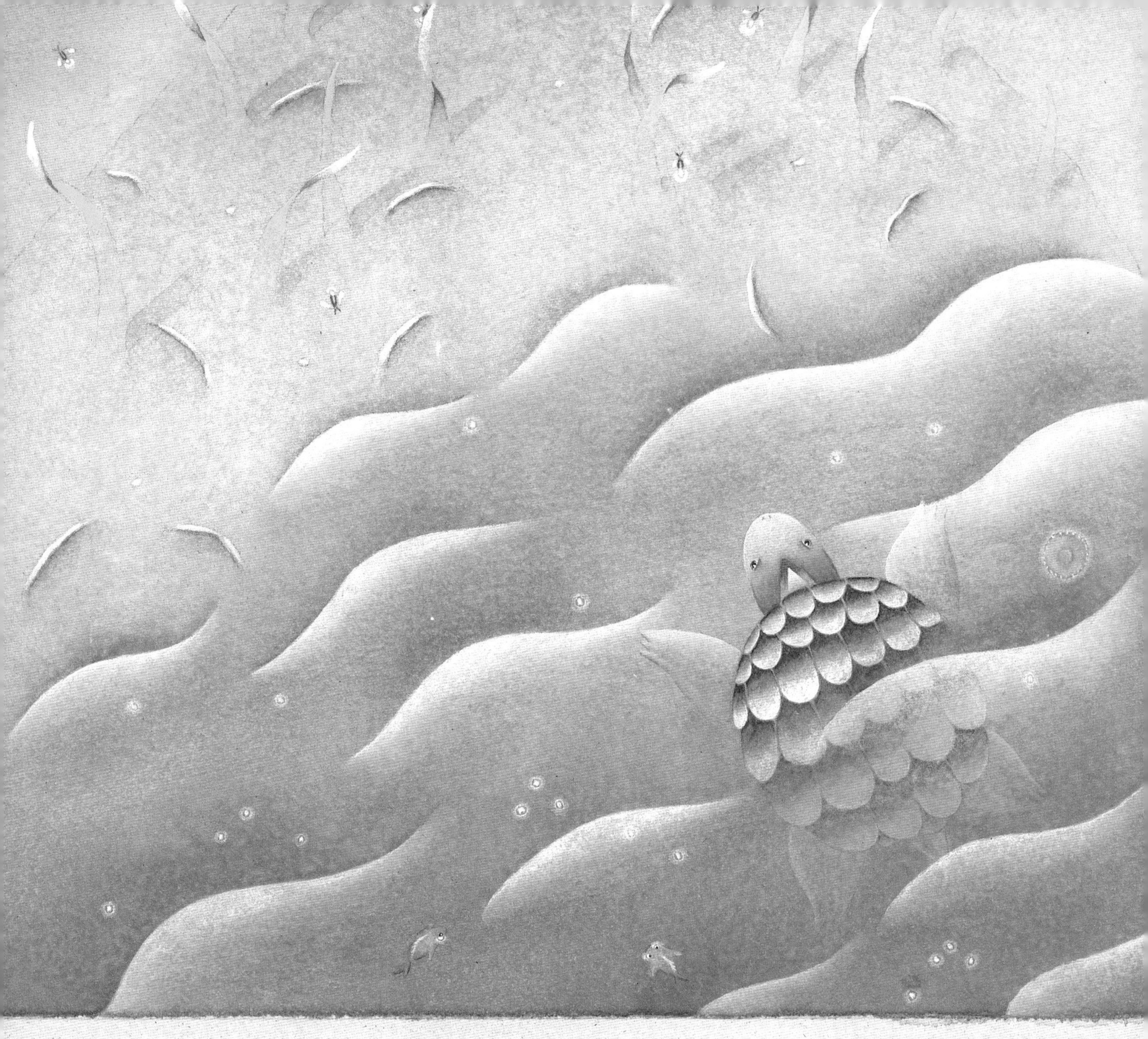

But then they remember to use all the twinkling lights to guide themselves home.

Safely nestled in, Bertie and Sandy tell their parents about the day's adventures, and how they had remembered what they were taught. Everything had been just as they had imagined it would be.

So Bertie and Sandy fall asleep, dreaming about tomorrow's adventures. And Mrs. Seabird whispers to Mr. Seabird, "It's been a **perfect** spring."